YOU ARE FANTASTIC!

SHORT STORIES FOR GIRLS ABOUT CONFIDENCE, FRIENDSHIP AND HAPPINESS! (PRESENT FOR GIRLS)

ANNABEL E. LEWIS

ISBN - 9798555296504

TABLE OF CONTENTS

INTRODUCTION

Stories are everything and have held such an important part in human history since the very beginning. That's why humans used to paint on the walls of caves, to help each other tell stories, and to share wisdom and knowledge. We wouldn't be where we are today without the beautiful stories we tell each other.

In this book, *YOU ARE FANTASTIC! Short Stories for Girls about Confidence, Friendship and Happiness! (Present for Girls)* we've collected a number of stories to help you be inspired to live a happy and fulfilling life and help you and your family to remember to focus on what's actually important in this world.

Within the following pages, you'll find genuinely original stories, stories inspired by some of your favorite classics, and adaptions of some of the most meaningful stories out there, all coming together and beautifully illustrated to help captivate you and your daughter, as well as sparking your imagination along the way.

We love these tales, especially the fact you can pick them up time and time again, and still find beautiful messages within the lines that can suit any and all situations you'll find growing up and dealing with different experiences.

Of course, go right ahead and enjoy the beautiful stories ahead, and if you do want them and get a lovely experience from them, it would mean the world to leave a review for this book where you purchased it. We love hearing your feedback, and positive comments inspire us to write more, so it keeps the cycle of storytelling in motion.

And with that, let's jump straight into our first story, a truly inspirational story that's all about how we all have the ability to look and share the beauty and love that's inside us, rather than just focusing on our physical appearances!

Enjoy your new stories, and we hope you'll discover a brand-new favorite you'll be itching to share with your family and friends!

STORY ONE:

THE GIRL WHO HAD NO TIME

Once, in a normal country in an ordinary world, there lived a girl who just wasn't happy with herself. Every morning, the girl would wake up before school and look herself up and down in the mirror.

"Urgh," she said to herself, "I hate my eyes look today," or other days she would say things like, "my hair just won't go right. I hate myself." One day, she woke up and really felt unhappy with how she looked, so badly that she didn't want to go to school.

She broke down in tears on her bed and refused to go to school.

"What's the matter, darling?" her mother said, coming to perch on the bed next to her daughter. The girl rolled over and laid her head on her mother's lap, and her mother stroked her hair gently.

"I'm so ugly, and I'm so horrible. Nobody wants to look at me. I don't even want to look at myself." The girl then broke out, crying harder than ever before.

Her mother pleaded with her daughter, telling her she was just as beautiful, if not more beautiful, than every other girl in the world. The daughter wouldn't listen and just wanted to be made beautiful.

Eventually, to get her daughter to go to school, her mother allowed her daughter to try some of her makeup, in the hopes of making her feel a little better about herself.

The girl, who had only ever tried the makeup in secret on the weekends without her mother knowing, felt her eyes light up. There was so much here to try and explore, from the skin shades of foundation to the most colorful lipsticks the girl had ever seen.

From that day onwards, the girl would always wake up in the morning, brush her teeth and her hair, would have breakfast, and then would spend most of her time before school putting on her makeup.

At school, everyone noticed the difference. While the girl used to be shy, quiet, and would usually keep to herself, she became one of the most popular girls in the school with her new-found confidence. She had new friends, the teachers liked her, and even a few of the boys would give her cheeky smiles as she walked around the halls.

Then, one day, the girl had a crazy dream. She tossed, and she turned in bed and had one of the worst night's sleep she had ever had. Because of this, she woke up late and didn't have so much time to do everything she usually did.

She brushed her teeth and her hair as fast as she could. She ate her breakfast in just four big mouthfuls, but still, she didn't have enough time to do her makeup.

"But Mom," she pleaded, "I can't go to school. I haven't done my makeup, and everyone is going to think I'm ugly and won't even look at me."

"Don't worry," her mother said, "I'll do your makeup for you really quickly right now."

And so the mother did her daughter's make up. The girl sighed a breath of relief. Her mother had done her own makeup for the many years now, so it made sense that she would be able to do it quickly.

Without a minute to spare, the girl kissed her mom on the cheek, careful not to smudge her lipstick, and ran out to the school bus, skipping as she went as her usual, happy self. She hung out with her friends, skipped across the playground, and smiled back at the boys who gave her a cheeky smile.

There was nothing strange about the day, and the girl got home from school in her usual happy self. However, when she went to the bathroom and saw herself in the mirror, getting ready to take her makeup off as she always did, her mouth dropped up.

There was not a single mark of makeup on her face. She searched high and low, pulling and her skin and getting as close up to the mirror as she could trying to find signs that she had worn makeup that day, but there was none.

She walked out to her mother, confused, and not sure what was on.

"My dear," she said, stroking her daughter's hair, "Being beautiful doesn't come from what makeup you're wearing or what clothes you have. It comes from inside you. You are beautiful on the inside. All the smiles and fun you had today, and have had every day, haven't come from your makeup. They come from you being you.

The girl smiled to herself, and was, from that day onwards, her beautiful self.

STORY TWO:

THE FROG IN THE PIT

There once was a pit in the woods that lived a family of frogs. Many of the frogs in the pit had lived there all their lives and knew nothing outside of the pit. And why would they? They had food from the bugs that flew into the pit, and their water puddles filled every time it rained. It was a simple life, and many of the frogs were happy with just the way things were.

However, there was one frog who dreamed of a better life—a life outside the pit.

"Don't be silly little frog. There's nothing out there for us. The grass is tall, and the trees taller. Some animals will eat you as soon as they see you. You're better off in the pit."

"But I want to see the tall grass and the taller trees," said the little frog, "I want to see all the beautiful and amazing things for myself. One day. I'm going to see it for myself."

The little frog was determined that one day she would make her dreams come true. A few months past and it was the middle of summer. The little frog woke up and looked up to the top of the pit and saw the summer sun shining down, warming her face. Today was the day.

The little frog had breakfast and did her chores, as she did every day, and then set off to the edge of the pit. With all her might, she pushed off from the ground and tried to grab the first ledge.

Just as she was about to grab on, she heard another frog call from down below.

"Little Frog!" the voice yelled out. "What are you doing? You can't jump out of it. It's impossible!" Hearing the words, the little frog missed the ledge and fell back down to the ground. Other nearby frogs hopped over to see what was going on.

"Little frog. There was a frog a few years ago, just like you, who tried to jump out of the pit. They got all the way to the top but missed the last ledge and fell all the way back down. He didn't make it, and I don't want the same to happen to you.

The little frog was sad. Yes, it was scary to try and jump out of the pit, and she didn't want to fall like the other frog. But at the same time, the little frog believed in herself and knew she could make the jump.

A few weeks later, the summer sun was shining, and the little frog knew that today was the day.

Once again, the little frog jumped up and grabbed the first ledge. This alone filled the little frog with determination to make it all the way. The little frog jumped from ledge to ledge and was so close to the top when she heard the other frogs calling from down below.

"Little frog, get down from there this instance! We've already spoken about this over and over again. You're going to get hurt."

Hearing the words from the other frogs, the little frog felt crushed. All the motivation and energy she had for fulfilling her dream of making it out and leaving the pit and fulfilling her destiny was gone, and instead, she was filled with an overwhelming sadness. She slowly climbed back down.

"Little frog," her mother said to her, "Why do you feel the need to leave the pit? Why not stay with us?"

"Because it's what I want to do. It's my destiny. I feel it deep within me that it's something I have to do. Why don't you believe in me?"

"We do believe in you, little frog. We just don't want you to get hurt."

The little frog sighed.

Why couldn't the other frogs just believe in her and help her make her dreams of seeing the big, wide world come true? Why couldn't they encourage her like they did her brother, who was to become an expert fly catcher, or her father, who was one of the best in the colony?

The little frog tried to let her dream go, and even though life in the frog pit carried on like it always had, the little frog couldn't shake her dream. It was something she had to do. She felt a spark inside her, brighter and bolder than any feeling she had ever had before. She knew in every cell in her body that this was something she had to do.

One morning, the little frog woke up bright and early set about going towards the edge of the pit. Just as before, she jumped to the first ledge, then the second and then the third, and eventually made it to the top.

She had never got this far before and had just one more ledge to jump. It was here when the little frog heard a cry from below. She looked down and saw all the other frogs were standing around the bottom of the pit and were shouting up something at her.

The little frog couldn't quite hear, but it sounded like they were encouraging her! Yes, they were! They were shouting things like "You can do it, Little Frog!" and "Yes, you can make it!"

Filled with the encouragement of her friends and family, the little frog gritted her teeth and made the final leap. She caught the edges of the ledge with her little hands and pulled herself out. At the top, the summer sun shone, and the world was even more beautiful than she had ever imagined.

Down in the pit, the other frogs who had been so scared for the little frog's safety were shocked. They hadn't been encouraging her at all but had been asking her to come back so she wouldn't hurt herself like they had been doing all the other times, but she had done it!

The other frogs were disappointed that they hadn't supported their friend's dream and wish they had been supportive from the beginning. All the frogs felt inspired to chase their dreams and make them become a reality because if the little frog could make her dreams come true, then they could too.

The little frog didn't even know. She waved and smiled at her friends and family below and thanked every single one of them for encouraging her to make it and helping support her to fulfill her dreams and went on to live a life happier than she had ever believed.

STORY THREE:

THE GIRL WHO SAVED A LIFE

There once were two friends, Sarah and Nicole, who had grown up as best friends from the day they were born. The girls had been born together in the same ward, their mothers were both friends, and they had spent nearly every day of growing up with each other.

They had done everything together and even went to the same school. They were the very best of friends. However, as the girls grew up and moved into high school, Sarah had started to change.

She started hanging out with new friends from the sports teams she was a part of and was becoming more and more interesting in boys and partying with the older students. Nicole wasn't interested in these things. She would much prefer to read her books, go for walks, and stay a bit quieter.

Nevertheless, despite growing up and liking different things, Sarah and Nicole still shared the same walk to school with each other as they always did. They left the house at the same time and walked along the river until they reached the school gates. Nowadays, this was the only time the girls really spent with each other.

Sarah wasn't like she used to be.

"Why do you always read books, Nicole? You should get yourself some friends. Maybe even think about getting a boyfriend." At least, this is how it started.

"Why do you wear your hair like you do, Nicole?" Sarah said one day, pulling at the bun so hard it actually hurt. Yet Nicole said nothing because she didn't want to seem weak in front of Sarah.

Over the years, these comments became a lot more hurtful. She said things like, 'I don't even know why I hang out with you anymore. You're a loser. You're nothing like me."

Nicole was obviously hurt by her long-term friend's comments, who was now seeming to change so much, but she didn't say a word. Instead, one night she went to speak about it to her father.

"Why is Sarah so mean to me? And to other girls as well. I've done nothing to her, and we used to be such good friends. I don't understand why things are so diffcrent."

"Well," her father said, "People change as they go through their lives, especially when you're so young still and trying to figure out what kind of person you are and what you stand for. It sounds like Sarah has become very caught up with her new friends and trying to be popular, even if that means keeping other people down."

Nicole was sad about these comments and just wanted things to go back to the way they were. "I hate it, dad," she said through tears. "I don't want to be friends with her anymore."

"You don't have to be Nicole darling," he said, "but the most important thing to remember is not to let Sarah get to you. She's just being someone and figuring out who she is, just like you are. She's on her own journey. I'm not saying she's a nice person, but you should forgive her for the horrible things she says and does."

"Forgive her?"

"Yes. If you hold on to a grudge and want to resent Sarah for what she has done, then what she does is only going to hurt you more and will make you upset for no reason. Just forgive her for any pain she causes and let it go."

Nicole only kind of understood what her father was saying, but knew she was feeling a lot of pain towards Sarah. However, instead of holding in the pain and getting upset by it, she listened to her father and tried her best to forgive Sarah and let it all go.

This was hard for the first few days. Sarah and Nicole still walked with each other to school every morning, and every day Sarah had a certain comment to make about something. Nicole took it, and instead of taking it in, she remembered that Sarah was on her own path of learning about herself, and while it wasn't nice, she just let it go.

However, come a week later, Nicole was given a choice. They were going to school together, as they always did, but winter had begun in their small town, and the path was icy cold. Walking along the river, suddenly Sarah slipped on a patch of ice and slid all the way down into the riverbed and was only moments away from hitting the ice-cold water!

For Nicole, everything went in slow motion.

She thought about all the horrible, nasty things that Sarah had been saying over the last few years and watched on as Sarah slipped down the bank and into the water. However, after a few moments, Nicole's father's voice popped into her head, reminding her that she wanted to be a good person, which means to forgive people for things.

In a snap second, Nicole threw herself down the bank after Sarah, and was only just able to grab her hand, her other hand grabbing onto a post that was stuck into the ground. Both the girls stopped sliding, and Sarah was just a foot from the water itself, the cold waters continuing to flow past.

The girls pulled each other back up to the main path, helped by other members of the public who also happened to be walking past at the same time on their way to work.

"Wow," said Sarah, clearly shaking from the experience. "You saved my life, Nicole, but I don't know why. I see that I have done and said so many horrible things to you over the years. I could have died then, and you saved my life. I don't know why you did it."

"I'm glad you see it now," said Nicole. "But I'm not going to hold a grudge against you for the horrible things you say. You need to figure out why you're a horrible person on your own, but I won't let your words hurt me. I am sad we're not friends like we used to be, though."

The girls talked it out on the way to school, and Nicole became a bit of a hero for saving Sarah and for her quick thinking. The girls decided to not walk together for a long time after that but are now friends now the Sarah is out of her phase of saying mean things to seem popular.

Nicole forgives her and is happy doing her own thing, free from the opinions of what others may think about her, glad that she can see herself as a good, kind person.

STORY FOUR:

THE CIRCUS ELEPHANT

Once upon a time, there lived a baby elephant in a dense jungle. The elephant had a happy life, playing around with the woods' animals, following her parents around the watering holes, and just generally having a nice life.

However, this all changed one day when humans came into the jungle one night and stole the baby elephant away while she was sleeping. Scary and alone, the baby elephant was bundled into a crate and transported around from person to person. While the elephant did not know where she was going, she knew she had been traveling for a long time and would now be far away from the jungle in which she grew up.

One day, after many weeks of traveling, the cloth over a cage she had been forced into was lifted, and she saw a massive rainbow-colored tent in front of her. She knew from her mother's stories that this was a circus, and she was to become an attraction.

Sad and confused, the elephant tried to escape back to her jungle each and every day. The circus trainers attempted to use food and treats to make her do tricks, but the elephant just wanted to go back home.

At night was the best chance to escape since there was nobody around, but the humans had tied the poor baby elephant up to a massive wooden pole that was stuck in the ground. The elephant pulled at the rope around her harness as hard as she could, but the pole would not move.

The pole was far too tall, far too wide, and stuck far too deep into the ground for her to move. She tried every night for weeks, and these turned into months, and eventually, years until finally, the elephant gave up.

She bowed down to the humans and performed their tricks and ate their food, and became one of the most successful acts in any circus for miles and miles around. No one had before seen such a beautiful and impressive elephant perform.

Years passed, and the elephant forgot all about her home in the jungle, and the circus had become her life. Every day she would wake up, eat, practice, go for a walk, and then perform in the evening. Then she would be tied up to her wood stake and would sleep until the morning, and then would do everything all over again.

The elephant was the star of the show, and everybody who saw her perform loved her. Her photo was copied onto all the posters for the circus, and even before the show started, the elephant from outside the main tent could hear the children asking when the elephant was going to come out.

While these comments made the elephant smile, and she enjoyed making people happy, she didn't like being in the circus against her will, as well as not being able to leave. She missed her family so much and knew her parents and friends, even now, many years later, would still be so worried about her.

One morning, however, the elephant woke up before anybody else in the circus had woken up. After stirring a while and then waking up properly, she realized she had been disturbed by a small rustling in the hay next to her.

She peered carefully through the darkness of the morning for a closer look and saw a tiny family of mice running past. They froze at the sight of her, but the elephant made it clear that she meant no harm.

"Don't worry, little mice," she said, trying to whisper as quietly as possible. "I won't hurt you. I just want to watch you for a while."

"Why do you want to watch us?" the oldest-looking mouse replied.

"Because I envy you so much. You get to run free and be wherever you want, whenever you want. You get to play and be free with your family and friends, and I don't get to have that. It makes me smile that you do."

The mice looked at each other and smiled. All the animals in the circus were locked up or kept in cages, and they were well and truly free to do as they pleased, for which they were very grateful.

"What are you doing here, mice?" the elephant said, "if you get caught here, the humans might capture you and make you a part of their circus, like me?"

"Don't be silly," one of the mice replied, "the humans aren't interested in creatures like us. Besides, I could ask you the same question. What are you doing here? Surely you should be off living wild in the jungle?"

"I wish I could," the elephant replied, "but I'm always tied up to this wooden pole for as long as I can remember. I tried for years to move it, but I never could. I'm going to be in this circus for life?"

The mice looked at the elephant, and then at each other and then laughed.

"What's so funny?" asked the elephant, genuinely curious to what they found so funny.

"You've tried pulling this stake? Have you looked at yourself, elephant? You are this giant elephant, bigger than any animal we've ever seen, and you can't pull out that tiny little stake?"

The elephant looked down at the stake, the same pole that had kept her tied to the same circus for so many years. The same pole she had pulled at time and time again while she was younger and hadn't touched in so many years.

As the mouse said, she had grown so much over the last few years, almost as be and as proud as her mother was, but the stake had not grown one bit. The elephant noticed this for the first time, and in doing so, wrapped her trunk around the pole and pulled.

Without any effort, the stake lifted from the ground, and the elephant couldn't believe what happened. She wandered around the field and felt no tug back. She was free to as she pleased and can't believe it had ever been so simple.

The mice looked her at smiling, sharing this truly happy moment with the elephant.

"Thank you so much," the elephant said. "I can't believe I gave up trying; even after many years of growing, I never thought to try and do the one thing I wanted more than anything in the world, and now I'm free."

The mice smiled and laughed, and all of them ran off into the fields together, leaving behind the circus and starting to find her way back home.

STORY FIVE:

THE BLIND GIRL

This is a tale about love and tragedy. When we go through life, many of us fall into the patterns of not being able to appreciate what we have when we have, and because we're so stuck in our ways, we fail to see the beautiful things that are in front of us.

Our story begins with a girl who was about 18 years old. She had spent her entire life blind in both eyes, and she hated herself for it. She had never been able to see the light of the sun, or the colors of the rainbow, or even the faces of her own family. She had never seen a smile, or a photograph, or rain dancing on the surface of a puddle.

She had never even seen the eyes of the boyfriend she had who loved her very dearly.

Every day was hard for the girl. She couldn't get around the house without bumping into things, and she had to walk down the street with a stick so she could feel where she was going. In school, she couldn't read the books like the other kids but had to listen to audiotapes or had someone next to her read for her.

Thankfully, her boyfriend made her life a lot better. He would always help her whenever it could and let her have independence at the same time.

"Why do you still date me?" she asked him one day. "I am blind, and my life is so hard. You could have such a better life if you were with a girl who could see."

"Because I don't want to be with any other girl," the boyfriend replied. "I love you just the way you are, and I wouldn't change anything for the world. You being blind is not who you are. The real you, the real you where vision doesn't matter, is the you I love."

"Well, I wish I wasn't blind, so I could see the sunrises and the sunsets, and I could watch all my favorite movies for the first time."

The boyfriend nodded but said nothing. Weeks turned into months, and the boy and the girl were still in love, just living their lives. One day, the boy took the girl for the most fantastic dinner date they had been on in their entire relationship.

"Hey," he started to say after they had finished their last course. "We've been together for a long time, and I was wondering, do you think that one day you would like to marry me? I would like to marry you."

The girl stopped and thought for a moment. The boy was a lovely boy. He was kind and caring, and everything a boyfriend should be, but she couldn't stop thinking about how much she hated herself and not being able to see.

"How about this," she replied. "If I can one day find a way to see, it is on that day I'll marry you."

The boy thought about her proposal and agreed.

A few months past and the boy heard about new surgery that was available that could help blind people see again. The girl was more excited than she had ever been. The sign-up process was long, but eventually, someone donated their eyes, and the girl was able to have the operation.

The operation was successful, and a few days later, she opened her eyes for the first time. She could see everything, and it was all so beautiful.

She saw the colors of the world, the trees blowing outside the window, and the warm white sunlight on her skin. She saw the faces of her parents and her boyfriend and couldn't help but feel happy.

This was until she noticed that her boyfriend had his eyes closed.

"Why won't you look at me?" she asked. "Why not open your eyes?"

"Today is the day you can see," the boy said, "so is this still the day you will marry me?"

"But why won't you look at me when you talk?" she said.

"Because I am blind, too," the boy replied. The girl burst out crying. Being blind was the most painful experience of her life, and she couldn't bear to spend her life with someone else who was blind. The girl refused to marry the boy and ran away from him in tears.

The boy, also crying, went home and felt incredibly sad about the whole situation. But, on the inside, he knew he had given the girl he loved the biggest gift anyone could ever give. The ability to see. It was all she had ever wanted.

One day, a few months later, he sat down to write a letter.

The letter read;

I hope you look after my eyes, dear soul. I will love you forever and always.

The girl received the letter and broke down crying. She had been able to see for months, and while everything looked beautiful, she had lost the boy he loved, and now she realized it was him who had donated the pair of eyes.

The girl noticed that life itself is a gift, whether she had a problem like not being able to see or not. Love still triumphs over everything, and she wished more than anything she could go back in time and just be happy with the boy, instead of just thinking about herself and then losing the most important thing to ever happen to her.

STORY SIX:

A PRESENT FULL OF KISSES

There once lived a very angry man who didn't enjoy his life. He went to work every single day in the same office with the same people he didn't enjoy spending his day with.

When the man was a child and grew up into a teenager, he had all these beautiful plans to be a writer. He wanted to write novels about the mystical and amazing worlds he had in his head, but life had gotten in the way, and he forgot something.

He ended up meeting a girl who he loved dearly, marrying her, and then having children. While he was happy, he never got to fulfill his dream. One day, he tried to write a book, but he never finished it, and the parts he did show people, they didn't really find as good as he hoped they did, so he gave up.

Over the years, the man felt as though the world was against him and didn't want him to be happy, and so he began to resent it. He resented himself and his life, and he tried to blame everyone for stopping him from living the life he wanted to live.

His daughter, a very beautiful girl who loved her father very much, felt very sorry for him and only wanted to see him happy.

On the weekends, when she wasn't at school, she would make him breakfast in bed, but he would only grunt while reading the newspaper, not really saying thank you. Other days, she would tidy up the house, so it was all nice and tidy when he got home because she knew that he loved the house being clean, but he always ignored it.

She tried different things over and over again, but nothing she did ever seemed to make him happy. Instead of trying new things, the girl decided to give him love. One evening, she bought a box home from school and spent all evening sitting in her bedroom, blowing kisses into the box.

When the box was full of kisses, she quickly closed it, so none would escape, and then wrapped the present up in beautiful gold and red paper, not unlike a Christmas present. She even wrapped it with a massive silver bow.

When her father came home that evening, she rushed over to the door to hand him his present. At first, the man was delighted to receive a gift, but soon his face gave away that he felt very disappointed.

"What is this?" he asked the girl. "The box is empty. There's nothing inside." The girl had to do everything she could to fight back the tears.

"But dad, it's a box of kisses. I blew hundreds in there for you."

The dad felt very bad about what he had said, and said sorry, saying he'll keep the present by his bed, so it's always nearby whenever he wants a kiss.

A few weeks past and tragically, the girl had an accident that took her life. The dad fell into even more sadness, and one night while he was going to bed, he found the box of kisses she had given him under the bed.

He opened it and took out one kiss and placed it very gently on his cheek. He sat thinking about his daughter had been the most amazing daughter in the world and was always doing things to make him happy. She tried so hard, and he never paid it any attention because he was always wrapped up in his own selfish ways.

Every night, he took another kiss out of the box from her and wished that he had been more grateful for the time they had together while his daughter was still around instead of holding onto the past.

From that moment on, the man dedicated his life to writing a book about his daughter's life and about how everybody should appreciate the time they have with their loved ones. The book became a bestselling, and he thanked his daughter every single day for helping him to realize his dream.

He did everything in her honor; she watched down on him from the heavens, happy to see that she had finally bought so much happiness into their relationship.

STORY SEVEN:

THE BOULDER IN THE ROAD

Ina. Far away kingdom in a distant time, there was a king who was really rather bored. Everything in the kingdom was running smoothly, and there was no drama or quarrels to deal with.

However, while everything was running well, he decided that he would take walks around his land to see what everyone else was up to. On his travels, he discovered something very interesting. Since times were good, everyone was becoming a little bit lazy.

Now, the king knew that lazy people in his kingdom was not a good place to be, and this meant things could go wrong very quickly, so he decided to test just how lazy people were.

Near the outskirts of town, he decided to place a large, heavy boulder he found in the woods in the middle of a road that many people used as they came and went from the main city. He then jumped into a nearby bush to see what happened.

Within a few minutes, the first horse and cart appeared a little way down the road. It traveled all the way up to the boulder, and instead of getting out and moving it, he instead pulled on the horse to take it around the outside. The king shook his head, disappointed.

About an hour later, one of the men who worked in his castle appeared, and the king knew he was returning home from seeing his family in another town. Like the first man, he approached the boulder, but instead of moving it out of the way, he simply rode his horse around the outside and carried on.

The king was still very disappointed in his castle man as he hoped he would have at least tried to move it so the path would be clear for anybody new coming into the kingdom. After all, a king has to make a good impression on new visitors to the kingdom.

The king stayed until the end of the day and came back the following days, and still, everyone simply avoided the boulder. They would either jump over the large rock if they were walking or would ride around if they were riding a horse.

It didn't even matter who the people were, whether they were commoners from the town or helpers in his grand castle; nobody bothered to move the boulder.

Finally, on the third day, just as the king was starting to believe that everyone in his kingdom had become so lazy, a farmer walked on and saw the boulder in the middle of the road. The king looked on, expecting to see the farmer wake past the boulder, just like everybody else.

However, the farmer did the unexpected without even stopping to look at how heavy the boulder was. He simply tipped it to the side and pushed it off to the side of the road, so it was entirely out of the way.

The king was shocked and jumped out of the bush before the farmer got back to the road. The farmer was clearly shocked to see the king of the kingdom he lived in suddenly standing face to face with him in the middle of a random road.

"My lord, I did not expect to see you here in the middle of nowhere. Are you okay?"

The king beamed the big smile for which he was famous.

"Of course, my humble farmer. I have sat here for three days waiting for someone who is not lazy to move this boulder from the road, and you have been the only person to do it! Here, this is your reward."

The king handed the farmer a large bag of gold, which wasn't small but enough to make him a fairly rich man for a long time.

"Thank you so much," the farmer said, "but why give me a bag of gold for moving a stone?"

"Because" said the king, "opportunities are everywhere in life, but so many people skip past them because they think there is nothing there, when in fact, there is so much we can do. You just have to be willing to go out and do it."

The farmer thought the king to be very wise and could see why he was king of all the land. And so, he took the bag of gold happily and went off to enjoy this new-found wealth.

STORY EIGHT:

THE TORTOISE AND THE BIRD

Once, there lived a very arrogant tortoise. The tortoise spent at least two hours every single day, making sure his shell looked its best. He would wash it down every single morning and every single night, and then would make it look beautiful by polishing it the best he could.

Then, once his shell was looking its best, he would march out into the woods to show off how amazing his home was. He would pass as many animals and their homes as he could, keeping his head high and never once looking at the homes of the others.

"Wow, look at that shell." he heard the rabbits say as they left their holes in the ground. "That is such a beautiful shell." The other rabbits agreed. The tortoise laughed to himself, as he would never have been seen living in a dirt hole like they did. So muddy. He much preferred his shell.

Next, he went down to the watering hole, where he saw the fish in the lake. The baby fish swam up to the tortoise, each one giggling with excitement about how beautiful the tortoise looked. The tortoise smiled to himself and shared with them the elaborate routine he had for making his shell the most beautiful.

All the fish, both children, and adults listened in awe, which made the tortoise feel very good about himself. When he was done, on he went with the rest of his day. Eventually, he came across the badger.

"Good Mr. Badger," the tortoise exclaimed, "May I ask you a question?"

"Of course," said the badger.

"I was wondering how you live in such a dirty, muddy hole? Surely it can't be nice living in the ground surrounded by nothing but dirt."

The badger looked very sad and upset with the tortoise's comment and didn't really know what to say.

"Well, I'm happy with it, and it's all I need and my family... I...."

The tortoise snorted to himself and left the badger, trying to find words to say. He continued on through the woods and eventually came to the next animal, the deer. There was a big herd of deer here, and many of them didn't even have a home. They just slept on the ground!

"Hey deer," said the tortoise. "Why don't you have a lovely home like my shell? Why do you choose to sleep on the ground and under bushes?"

The deer snorted to themselves. "We will admit that your shell is something amazing, and I haven't seen a shell as beautiful as it, but we are deer, and we don't need a shell, nor a home. We are one with the forest and can sleep wherever we please in safety."

"But would you not like a beautiful shell-like mine?"

"While it would be great, we cannot have one."

"No, you cannot," said the tortoise. He smiled to himself as he thought about all the animals that could not even think about having a shell as amazing as his shell, which made him even happier. If nobody else could have a beautiful shell, then he would always be special.

The tortoise spent the rest of his day, as he did most days, roaming around the forest, checking in with all the animals, showing off his shiny shell.

However, late in the afternoon, he came across a somewhat random collection of twigs on the ground and went over to see what it was. As he got closer, a little bird jumped out of the circle, and the tortoise soon realized this was actually the bird's nest.

"Oh my," said the tortoise, clearly taken aback. "Your nest, your home, it's so raw and dirty and messy. I don't understand how you could live in such a horrible way. Look at how beautiful and elegant my shell is. Wouldn't you like to live in a home-like this?'

The bird thought for a moment before replying.

"Yes," the bird said, "your home is very beautiful, but it has one problem. You see, there is only room in your home for just you. Here in my nest, I have room for all my family and friends. While my house may be messy, it holds all the people I love. Where are all the people you love?"

The tortoise thought for a moment and then thought about everyone he had met throughout the day. The rabbits. The fish. The badgers. All of them lived in messy homes, but they all lived together in one big house with the people they loved. The tortoise was alone.

"Look," said the bird, "You don't need to be upset. Just remember that looks aren't everything in life, and you can't go around thinking that you are more beautiful than everyone else and trying to put everyone else down. To you, how your shell looks may be the most important thing in the world to you, and that's okay. To me, the family is the most important thing, not the state of my home or how beautiful it is."

The tortoise thought for a moment and realized the bird was right. Looks can be nice, but they weren't the most important thing. And so, the bird invited the tortoise to come and stay for dinner and then spent the next day helping the tortoise find his family and friends, so he didn't have to be alone in the woods anymore.

DISCLAIMER

This book contains opinions and ideas of the author and is meant to teach the reader informative and helpful knowledge while due care should be taken by the user in the application of the information provided. The instructions and strategies are possibly not right for every reader and there is no guarantee that they work for everyone. Using this book and implementing the information/recipes therein contained is explicitly your own responsibility and risk. This work with all its contents, does not guarantee correctness, completion, quality or correctness of the provided information. Misinformation or misprints cannot be completely eliminated.